PRESIDENT PENNYBAKER

Kate Feiffer · illustrated by Diane Goode

A Paula Wiseman Book
Simon & Schuster Books for Young Readers
New York   London   Toronto   Sydney

FOR BUMMA—K. F.
FOR PETER—D. G.

SIMON & SCHUSTER BOOKS FOR YOUNG READERS · An imprint of Simon & Schuster Children's Publishing Division · 1230 Avenue of the Americas, New York, New York 10020 · Text copyright © 2008 by Kate Feiffer · Illustrations copyright © 2008 by Diane Goode · All rights reserved, including the right of reproduction in whole or in part in any form. · SIMON & SCHUSTER BOOKS FOR YOUNG READERS is a trademark of Simon & Schuster, Inc. · Book design by Lucy Ruth Cummins · The text for this book is set in Pike. · The illustrations for this book are rendered in watercolor. · Manufactured in China · 10 9 8 7 6 5 4 3 2 1 · Library of Congress Cataloging-in-Publication Data · Feiffer, Kate. · President Pennybaker / Kate Feiffer ; illustrated by Diane Goode. – 1st ed. · p. cm. · "A Paula Wiseman book." · Summary: Tired of the unfairness of life, young Luke Pennybaker decides to run for president, with his dog Lily as his running mate. · ISBN-13: 978-1-4169-1354-2 (hardcover) · ISBN-10: 1-4169-1354-8 (hardcover) · [1. Politics, Practical–Fiction. 2. Humorous stories.] I. Goode, Diane, ill. II. Title. · PZ7. F33346Pr 2008 · [E]–dc22 · 2007004815

first edition

On a not too sunny but not too cloudy, not too hot but not too cold
Saturday afternoon in May, Luke Pennybaker asked his father one
question because Luke Pennybaker wanted just one thing.

"Dad," he said, "can I watch TV?"

His dad didn't say yes, as Luke thought he should have.

And he didn't say no, as he usually did when Luke asked him if
he could watch TV.

Instead he answered Luke's one question with five entirely
different new questions.

Luke thought that was unfair because one question
deserved one answer, not five more questions.

"Did you clean your room?

"Did you eat your lunch?

"Did you brush your teeth this morning?

"Did you feed the fish?

"Did you ask your mother if she needs help with anything?"

"No, no, no, no, no," answered Luke. Then he asked again, "So, can I watch TV?"

This time his dad gave him just one answer. "NO!"

So Luke Pennybaker cleaned his room, ate his lunch,
brushed his teeth, fed the fish, and asked his mother if
she needed help with anything.

Then he went back to his father with his one question. "Dad, now can I watch TV?"

Luke Pennybaker's father looked at his son and said . . . "NO."

It was at this very moment, this precise instant, this exact time and place that Luke realized life was unfair.

A few moments later—after Luke yelled as loud as he could and was sent to his room—he decided that he would do whatever he could to make life fair.

And so goes the story of how Luke Pennybaker became the youngest boy ever to run for president.

Luke went to school that Monday and announced his candidacy.

"Please vote Pennybaker for president," he said.

"I promise to make life fair.

"I promise that if I'm elected president, you'll only have to do homework when you want to.

"I promise that if I am elected president, you'll be able to eat dessert any time of the day and go to sleep as late as you want to.

"I promise that if I'm elected president, every child in America will get a dog or a cat or a hamster or a gerbil or a rabbit or an iguana."

The children in Luke's school all cheered, "Pennybaker for president!"

That week they set up a campaign office and named
Luke's dog, Lily, as the vice presidential candidate.

They put up posters and called their cousins, asking
them to send their pennies to the Pennybaker for President
campaign.

Luke and Lily spent the summer traveling around the country, campaigning.
They campaigned on top of a mountain in Colorado

and on the beach at the Jersey shore.

They campaigned in a candy store in Kansas

and at a dog show in Detroit. (The rest of Luke's family came too,
but they were just vacationing.)

On a campaign stop in New Hampshire, a reporter asked Luke what party he was in.

"Luke, are you in the Democratic Party or the Republican Party?"

Luke replied, "I'm in the Birthday Party."

He told the reporter that in the Birthday Party kids get treated like it's their birthday every day of the year. They get to eat cake and ice cream and open presents every morning. They get to wear shorts in the winter and dirty clothes to fancy parties. They get to play games at school and draw pictures during dinner. They can flood the bathroom when they take a bath and keep their room as messy as they want to.

Later that summer, at a campaign stop in Iowa, a reporter asked Luke what was the first thing he would do as the youngest president in America.

Luke replied, "Paint the White House orange."

The other presidential candidates were asked what they thought about Luke's idea. One of the candidates said she thought the White House should be painted blue. The other candidate thought it should be painted red.

But Luke liked orange. And it seemed like the rest of the country did too.

By late summer Luke and Lily were leading in the polls.

Lily was named most popular pup in the country.

"Happy Birthday" became America's most-sung song.

"We're tired of the unfair! We want Pennybaker for president! Bark for the Birthday Party!" roared the crowds.

To show his support, the current president bought 40 gallons of orange paint and started to paint the White House. When he ran out of paint, he bought 40 more gallons and 40 more and then 40 more. By November the White House was painted orange.

On election morning Luke went to cast his vote but was told he couldn't vote because he was too young.

Luke went on TV to point out how unfair it was that he was not allowed to vote. Lily stood by his side and barked because she hadn't been allowed to vote either.

"We'll vote for you," said the voters.

Luke and Lily won the election by a landslide.

In January, President Luke Pennybaker and Vice President Lily Pennybaker moved into the orange White House and ordered cake, ice cream, and presents for every person and bones for every dog in America.

But the mayor of New York didn't like her present.

And a senator in Maine was allergic to ice cream.

And the governor of California wouldn't eat anything with sugar in it.

And the dog of a city councilman in Cincinnati refused to chew on his bone.

And the phone started ringing. And Lily wouldn't stop barking. And everyone wanted to talk to President Pennybaker. They needed him to come here and go there, and look at this and talk about that. And all President Pennybaker wanted to do was watch TV and ride his bicycle and read his books and play with his toys. He even wanted to clean his room, eat his lunch, brush his teeth, feed the fish, and help his mom. But he couldn't because he was far too busy being president.

It wasn't fair.

So after his first week of being president, the youngest president in history stepped down.

"I want to do what's fair," he said.

He packed his bags and left the orange White House.

As he walked away, he turned around and looked back.
The new president was sitting near a window, looking out at
Luke. Luke waved and yelled, "Good luck. I know you'll be fair."

The new president nodded, picked up her paw, and barked back.